ALL THESE UNQUIET SOULS

AN ARKLE WRIGHT NOVELLA

RAYMOND S FLEX

1

THE STAR UP ABOVE just about baked my blood and I could feel my heart lubbering about, working its way slowly further up into my throat. The sand, though, the pissing sand. That was the worst of it by far. The way it streamed right in through both nostrils and somehow through my lips pressed hard together, turning my mouth into some kinda mini desert.

No bloody taste in my mouth yet, though, and that was the one to look out for. I knew that once I tasted blood in my mouth I was liable to passing out. And I could still smell the desert wind, too, and its grainy texture as it blew up against my cheeks.

That same wind, why it just howled all about me, whipping up the sand dunes, snapping the sand on its gusts something like a common-place whip. And it lashed me, against the back of my uniform, and got all stuck in the sweat soaking my skin.

I guessed I looked something like a snowman stuck in a sandstorm, and I was melting awful quick.

I clutched my blaster rifle tighter to my chest and screwed up my eyes against the bright daylight. To be honest, I was building up a pretty profound and shitty-stomached hatred for Asfarth-14, oh I hadn't that much against the planet itself, to be sure, but the swilling sand that blew off its surface, the deserts covering pretty much every square centimetre of the place. Yeah, that was something I couldn't much abide by.

But training's training and, being a fourth-year officer in the Fritten System Authorities, I couldn't much let up or allow a bunch of sand to get me all pissy. Then again, I was muttering more than my fair share of swearwords under my breath as I continued to stalk on across the ever-shifting sand, feeling my boots sinking into it just about every step.

My calf muscles were more than on fire, they felt just like molten lead by now. And as for my feet, why they were Blister City right about then, and I kept gettin' these feverish visions of my feet, snugged up inside my boots, and the blisters popping one by one. Warm puss getting my socks all soggy and stinky.

What I wouldn't have given for a water canister.

Nah, scratch that, I probably woulda sold the boots off my feet for a *drop* of water. And for all the good they were doin' for my battered-old feet that mighta been not-too-dumb a deal.

The water thing was a problem though, truth be told. I'd gone and run out of water a day or so ago. I was runnin' on less than empty. Not on the point of death, let's not get melodramatic here.

Speaking bluntly, though, I was in a bunch of trouble.

But I bucked on, good little soldier I was, keeping my blaster rifle clutched tight to my body, and trying not to think too much about the heat coming off the star . . . whatever the *hell* its name was . . . as it melted my brains through my thicker-than-average skull.

Had to keep goin'.

Just had to.

Maybe I'd stumbled on for a few more minutes, maybe it'd just been another few seconds . . . or—who knows?—maybe it'd been several hours. Just like I said, my brain was well and truly fried, and I couldn't see straight, let alone *think* straight.

But I gave it a shot anyway . . . the *seeing* straight.

I held my hand up to my eyebrows, so stuck with sweat now that they were like a pair of tiny, but very absorbent sponges. In fact, as I laid the back of my hand up against them, I was sure that I felt a good helping of sweat squidge right out from them, and those salty droplets roll their way down my face, adding a little ticklin' to the lashing I was getting from the sandy, swilling winds.

Narrowed eyes, and the hand shielding the worst of the bright star beating down on me, got me as far as seeing about fifty or more metres in any direction.

Dunes, as far as the eye could see.

Bustling, ever-moving, shifting, sand dunes.

Just then my throat seemed to reach critical mass on account of all the sand I was breathing into my mouth, and I swallowed it down, not thinking too straight.

Most likely the worst mistake I'd made all day.

Almost straight away I felt that rough feeling inside me, like someone was giving my guts a good seein' too with sandpaper and, I guess, in way, that was just what was happening.

Why don't *you* try swallowing some sand, just a little, and see how it leaves you?

And so, with a bunch of retching but no vomiting, like I said, I just didn't have the liquids to account for anything like that, I stumbled over and fell into the sand, right down there in a heap.

I remember staring up into the sky, into that thick, greenie atmosphere, and I was almost certain, just for a second or so, that I could see the stars twinkling down on me from the midnight blue of space. I was almost convinced that I could see my future, right up there, stretching out above me.

What did I see right up there, in the stars a blinkin' and a twinklin'?

Well, that's just what you're about to get to finding out.

———

First thing's I noticed lying there, on the sand, feeling it all puffing up about me, and occasionally conspiring into little zephyrs and spitting against my cheeks, was the gentle *throb* and *hum* beating about above my head.

I just about had the strength to shift my muscles, to get them into some kinda logical sequence, and I got to seeing the sand all swill up again.

At first I thought I was seeing stuff, or *hearin'*, stuff, something like that, and my next thought was that a mighty, great sandstorm was just blowin' on its way, come to finish me off.

And that's when I got to thinking about gods, and stuff like that. And wondered if this planet, if this ugly great desert planet, Asfarth-14, if it might have something that we'd never seen in such a way or anything.

But, no, and probably for good reason, the

noise wasn't a sandstorm kicking up a fuss at all. No, it was an Extractor sent on down from the good old *FSA-0100T*—the mother ship.

Finally, and not before time, they'd come down here to pick me up.

I'd have liked to say that I was all burly and masculine about it. But the truth like it happened, well, it was more like I got a little dewy-eyed . . . *jus'* a little . . . as I watched those reverse thrusters pound down against the sand all around me, and the suction tube linger right there above me.

And next thing I knew I was being vacuumed up, saved from this bleak little shit-stain on the face of the universe.

Goin' back home.

Or at least to home as I now knew it.

2

T HERE AIN'T many better sights in the whole stretch of the universe than Sheila Mutely, Ship's Doctor of the *FSA-$0100T$*, unwinding her stethoscope, untangling it from that white-blond hair of hers, and then blowing just a little of her wonderful warm breath on the metal suction cap thingy to take the biting chill away.

At least I thought as much, lying up there, in the medbay on the *FSA-$0100T$*. Just like all medbays it had that crunchy—kinda crispy—paper lying beneath my pert and peachy bum cheeks, and whenever I moved a muscle it crackled away.

If my feet were well-acquainted, if not

life-long tenants of Blister City, then my mouth was definitely searching out a good mid-sized investment in downtown Sand City. And, to be honest, pain was just about flushing its way through every last nerve and bone of my body, not that I was gonna show anything less than a hardy, teeth-gritted grin to Doctor Mutely.

As she leaned over me, those crystalline, blue eyes of hers somehow drifting off into space, her hair rubbed against my bare chest. Only then, watchin' her press that stethoscope up against my ribcage, did I realise how much sand had actually got inside of my uniform. In fact, taking a proper good look at my chest, I saw that there was just about more sand than skin sticking to me.

I gotta good sniff of that clean smell of Doctor Mutely. Unlike all the other doctors I've run into over the years, she managed to somehow get a handle on that twisted, sterile scent that just seems to follow anyone connected in any way with the medical profession.

And, let me tell you, that smell just twists my gut.

So I felt pretty fortunate to have run across someone like Doctor Mutely.

Her hands, too, all those delicate fingers of hers that seemed just so perfectly coordinated as she went about her exam, working practically, efficiently, not stopping to wander as she tapped her fingers here and there, and then, as I felt a pretty meaty sigh rock my shoulders, she drew back and hung up her stethoscope about her neck.

"Officer Wright," she said. "How're you feeling?"

"Why, I'm feeling just fine."

She gave me a tiny little nod and I realised, just as I always seemed to do whenever I saw her again, that she was pretty petite, nothing big about her. And that the way she wore her medical jacket dangling over her, several sizes too big, gave the illusion that she was much bigger than she actually was.

I guess having to work on a ship like the FSA-o1ooT that was just about par for the course. How else was she supposed to get herself taken seriously without a little physical bulk? Why, the whole of the FSA, or any army for that matter, just about relies on a those shows of strength.

They all add up, and brute strength is never —*ever*—to be underestimated.

Not to say that I've ever been one to throw my weight round, though I know just who I'd back in a bar fight, jus' as long as I haven't drained the bar dry of moiser, that is . . . and those days, back in the FSA, things were pretty different and all. What with the tests they made us all take. With the way they checked our blood—our piss—for any traces of drugs or alcohol. To be honest, I'd been takin' more than a little care, because if there was one thing that I just wouldn't be able to stand, it would be getting sent back to Arkle-4, back to my home planet.

Back to Bomberlee City.

No way was I goin' back to Bomberlee.

Nah, once you've left Arkle-4 there's one thing that's for sure. You'll never—*ever*—go back there willingly. Yeah, I might blab my mouth time to time about the multitude of other shitty planets in the universe, but noth-ing, and I mean *nothing*, compares to my own home planet.

When it comes to shitty planets, I know what I'm talking about. Just trust me on this one, all right?

Doctor Mutely got herself all busied with the readouts beside the examination table I was lying down on, and I just watched her, out the corner of my eye. And, I'm not ashamed to say it, I was trying my best to catch her eye, to have her look back at me, and maybe show me one of those nervous grins of hers that I'd been hearing good things about from the boys round the ship.

But, no dice.

"Officer Wright," she said, again sending a quiver through me with that cold, professional tone of hers, "it's going to take you most of the night to get yourself rehydrated."

She nodded to the needle sticking out of my arm, the one I'd pretty much forgotten all about since I'd been spending most of my attention on the good doctor.

The liquid itself, which I watched surging, bubbling, its way through the transparent tube, was a light green colour. It reminded me of one of those drinks I used to get back home, back on Arkle-4, it'd been called Snarple Crank, and had been so stuffed of sugar and preservatives, and God knows what else, that back at school it had this reputation so bad, so *wicked*, that it became like a game.

Whenever any kid there, at school, got their hands on some money, or whatever, we'd all buck on down to the shop on the corner and order us a litre of Snarple Crank. That stodgy, lime-coloured mixture of stuff, and then we'd each take a sip from it, take turns drinking it down.

I can still remember all the crackling in my mouth that it did, how it left my tongue something like a dehydrated sausage, all sizzled out in a frying pan. And that was to say nothing of just what it did to my gut. Why, it just about turned it inside and out, and I can still remember how my mum would batter her fists against the toilet door wanting to know just what the hell was taking so long in there.

Snarple Crank, yeah, now that's a mind rush if ever there was one.

As I lay there on the examination table, I did notice Doctor Mutely shift her gaze onto mine. Well, praises be praised, I couldn't believe it when she did it. I could never remember a time when any one of my buddies who'd gone in for an examination with her actually came back out with a credible story of actually getting some eye contact off her.

But, look at me now, because that was just what was happenin'.

Imagine my all-out surprise and wonderment when she raised that eye contact with a wry smile, and then said, "Word is on the ship that you broke the record down there by more than twice the time."

As I rested there on the examination table, actually having just about clear forgot where I'd just been, that I'd been taking part in a one-man survival training exercise, I just blinked pretty vacant-like a few times.

Her smile widened. "It took the Extractor a long while to track you down, and they said you'd pounded out a good five hundred klicks from the drop-off point. Guy I spoke to said that the brass had never heard of anything quite like it. They were almost certain they were going to turn up a corpse down there."

It felt like someone had hollowed out my chest, and that I was floatin'. I almost totally lost myself in those eyes, in those crystalline, dazzling blue eyes, but I somehow managed to keep my composure. Maybe it was the calming effect of whatever they had jabbed into my veins, but more likely it was the good doctor's creamy smile.

"Don't know much about that, ma'am, all's I know is that I was just tryin' to stay alive, you know? Jus' taking things one step at a time, one hour at a time. That's all you can do, I reckon."

She adjusted that smile of hers into a wry smirk then broke off the eye contact and looked back to my readouts in the machine at the side of the examination table. "Good thing they found you when they did, though. Another hour or two and you'd have been a pretty smoked rasher of bacon."

"That so?" I said, sounding way more gung-ho about it than I truly felt.

She flashed her eyebrows and gave me another dose of those mesmerising eyes of her. When she spoke her voice was crisp and cool. "Oh yeah."

3

MUCH TO MY UPSET, Doctor Mutely soon withdrew from the examination room. I guess she had to go take a nap, or go get some food, something like that. The upshot of the whole deal was that I was just laid out there, still on that examination table, getting all dosed up with that rehydration stuff.

The machine churned away beside me, making this tiny, nasal mechanical *whine*, the kinda whine that I'm told often sends prisoners round the bend, makes them kill their bunkmates and the like just to get sent to solitary so as they don't have to hear it no more.

Now that Doctor Mutely had left my presence, I found myself getting all caught up with thoughts of that Snarple Crank all over again, getting those reminiscences coming thick and hard, playing out all over my mind.

And whenever I got those tingling sensations at the back of my mouth, that stomach-quibbling sensation shot on my mind, then I'd just think back to the sand again. And I'd feel it still rattling all about my chest, like it'd got trapped in my lungs, and that it was gonna sting me till the day I died.

At least Doctor Mutely 's sweet scent continued to linger for a while, there in the stifling, recycled air of the examination room. And I found myself pining for her, wanting her to come back. But, when I next heard the door to the examination swish back it wasn't Doctor Mutely darkening the doorway, but a captain. Not one I recognised, to be sure, but I surmised his rank from the patches stuck to his chest, and the stitched on rings coiled about the cuffs of his uniform.

He was all-told about ten or so years older than me, which placed him in about his mid-thirties. And that age also told me that he was a junior captain, hadn't put all that much into his profession. At least not yet. And, I guess, that put me a little at ease with him, despite the difference in our ranks.

He wore his cap pressed hard down over his head, so that it had the effect of making his ears jut outwards. The ratio of his cheekbones to eyes also bothered me a little. His cheeks were all squishy, while his eyes were almost like tiny little pinpricks, kinda afterthoughts in the rest of his face.

My eyes just about wandered over his name badge, took it in, before he spoke to announce himself.

"Officer Wright?" he said, and then took a step forwards, into the examination room, and thrust out his hand for me to take. "Name's Captain Hughes."

Well, I just about glared at that hand as if it was some foreign *thing*, and then, realising that he was givin' me a kinda weird look, I decided to shake his hand before he got ideas that I'd gone all gooey in the brain down there on Asfarth-14.

He had a firm shake, and my hand was way flimsier than I'd expected. I guess going through that survival routine down there in the desert had kinda taken its toll on me. And now it made sense to me that Doctor Mutely had been impressed that I'd managed to survive down there for twice as long as anyone else.

"Pleased to know you, skipper," I said, unable to keep the kick out of my voice, in that wound-up habit way I sometimes have. Like I thought before, it was most likely because he wasn't all that much older than me and, for a captain, younger than most.

Captain Hughes kinda made his nose twitch in a way that reminded me of a rabbit, and then he averted my eyes and looked to the machine ticking along beside the examination table. He tilted his head towards it as if to say, 'Do you mind?'

Why should I have cared? I was just an army runt ready to throw his body on the line for the FSA, and so I nodded him through.

He strutted up to the readouts and jutted out his lower lip in a pout, almost as jutted out as those ears at the side of his head. "It's true then," he said, still fixed on the readouts.

"What's true?"

He slipped me a sidelong glance. "That you're a hardy soul, not all that shook up by that experience you had down there, planetside."

"And what *experience* is that . . . Captain?" I added, after a brief pause, realising that my tone had been not a little sharp, and remembering my manners, even if this guy was just a fledgling captain.

He caught my glare a little, wrestled the bite out of it and then smirked.

I guess there mighta been a little more to this guy than met the eye. But then, thinking about it, for someone to make captain at his apparent young age, they'd surely have to show a little bite themselves.

"You know," he continued, "getting blown about down there, in the sandstorms. D'you know how many people we've lost down there over the years?"

"Not a clue, Captain."

"Yeah, well, you're best off not knowing." He paused a moment, and I'm sure that I saw a sparkle, a *gleam* in his eye right then. "It'd only go to your head."

I brought my hand up to my temple and gave it a rub. I squinted at the captain, still standing over there by my readouts. "Can I help you with something, *Cap*-tain?"

He shrugged and then glanced off in the direction of the door, as if he'd heard footsteps outside, someone ready to enter the examination room. I met his gaze on the way back from the door. "Gotta proposal for you."

"Oh yeah?" I said. "And what's that when it's at home?"

He snorted what I think was supposed to pass as a laugh then said, "You've picked up your desert survival training, and way things have been it's come to my attention . . . that is, I couldn't help noticing reading over the latest officer lists, that you've come through quite a few scrapes, got yourself commended a good few times."

"Yeah, and what of it?"

"Well," he said, a slight firmness entering his voice, "I was thinking that you might well make a good lieutenant on some ship."

Now there're some things that you've just got to flat laugh at, and this was one of those times. And so, maybe because of the rehydration stuff gushing through my system, or perhaps because I was not a little weary following my beating all other training records out the water, but I cranked my head right back and, up against that flimsy pillow, I laughed out long and hard.

When I got myself back under control, I rolled over on my side, taking care not to dislodge that tube of mine, and I looked him in the eye.

Sweet Jesus, the man was serious.

Actually serious.

He just shot me back that badass, young-captain, steely glare, the one that I was sure could burn its way right through my eyeballs . . . and straight into the back of my skull, if I wasn't careful about it.

"I want you to think about it, Wright. It could be an excellent opportunity for you."

Now it was dawning on me that this captain was actually serious, that this proposal of his *was* actually serious. I tried to get some composure back, to rock myself into some kinda normal way, and then I said, "What're you flyin' anyway?"

"Pelter."

Despite the more serious façade I was trying to get across, I couldn't help a long and flat-toned whistle. "Why, Captain, that must be some serious action."

"That's why I thought you might be the man for the job."

I propped myself up a little more on my elbows and eyed the captain closely, trying to get beneath the surface of his there eyes.

Flat, matted, almost unfeeling.

Ruthless.

I knew this was a man to trust, a man who knew just what he wanted and would do whatever it took to get it.

And right then, right at that moment, he wanted me.

But I knew how to play that game too, how to take a spin on the dance floor with the rest of the brass, and so I kept my cards close to my chest, tried not to let go of my enthusiasm, of something inside me letting rip, telling me that this might be my big chance to make a splash in the FSA.

Everyone would be watching this appointment.

"Captain," I started, "you know as well as I do how this whole thing works, you know just what we signed up for here." I picked out his gaze again, then continued, "And you know that if the FSA ask me to jump, all's I can say is 'How high?'"

"So, what're you sayin'?"

I screwed up my eyes a little, thinking over how what the captain had last said sounded kinda familiar. I looked him square in the eyeballs then said, "Where're you from exactly, you know, in the universe?"

The captain shrugged. "Arkle System."

Pretty much without even thinkin' about it, a smile crossed my lips. "That so?"

"Yeah, I shook the accent pretty good." He gave me a dour nod, then added, "Sounds like you're already well on the way to doin' that too." He shrugged. "Can help a career, that's all I'm saying."

Guess that just what Captain Hughes said had some sense to it. But, like I'd already figured it, I wanted to stay neutral for the time being, wait things out, just a little.

"Be in touch, Officer Wright?" he said, holding out his hand again.

I took his hand off him and gave him a real shake this time. "Sure will be."

He gave me one of those stern grins, the

ones that I'd seen from time to time back on Arkle-4, the ones that the tough kids—the ones that *survived* without turning into addicts or whatever else—wore when they walked the streets.

It was a smile that showed they wouldn't be shaken, no matter what.

And I knew, without looking in the mirror, that it was my own smile.

4

BLESSED BE THE . . . whatever the hell's playin' at ruling this universe that Doctor Mutely shoved on in about five minutes after Captain Hughes had marched himself back out of the examination room. At least it only seemed five minutes to me, but maybe I slept. I was that tuckered out.

While she scanned the readouts, I checked out her figure, the one that was near enough hidden by that baggy doctor's coat of hers.

Guess a guy can't have all the luck in the universe in one day.

"You're clean to go," she said, without looking round.

I guessed she was just slipping back into

protocol, back to her normal duties. And I wasn't a patient no longer, no concern of hers. And so I shifted myself off that crackling paper cover of the examination table and dropped to the floor.

The floor itself was just a little cold against the soles of my feet. And, as it turned out, those blisters hadn't taken any of that rest I'd been dosing myself with. The pain flashed up my calves, and then tingled right up my spine. But I managed just to keep it down to a manly grunt, since I didn't want Doctor Mutely to think me some wuss who'd somehow got lucky.

I stared at the doctor's back a good five seconds, lingered far too long on that ever-clean blond hair of hers, and that sweet odour. And then I told myself that playtime was over, and that I had places to be, I had missions to accept.

When I reached the door, and my hand was lingering out in mid-air, ready to punch the button which would deactivate the lock, the doctor spoke to me, without turning round, apparently busying herself with the readout machine, getting ready for the next patient.

"Your clothes are all back on your bunk, all been cleaned up pretty nicely, or so I hear it."

My voice stuck in my throat, got all low and gravelly, *cracked* almost. "Thanks," I said.

"Don't mention it," she said, and then glanced back over her shoulder, her eyes meeting mine, and then said, "Seemed the least I could do to send them off to Laundry while you were getting some rest."

"I appreciate it."

"I had a quick look over your history, your *service* history, and it seems that you've been no stranger to medbays while you've been in the FSA."

Now, usually, that's something that I'd love to have a boast about. And if I'd been down in my bunk, with the other dozen guys I bunked with, I woulda been quick to confirm that. But now, standing here in the examination room, and with the sorta weedy way that she spoke it, the way she stated it, it made me think that really it was nothing to be proud of at all.

Or, worse, that I'd been pretty lucky so far.

Even despite all that, I managed a, "Sometimes shit happens, y'know?"

She gave me a kinda flinching grin, and the slightest-ever lift of one of her eyebrows. I wondered if she was gonna add something else, because I was almost certain she was. The way that her eyes lingered over mine, and the way that her lips were parted just enough for me to see the saliva glimmering on the tip of her tongue. But, no, she had nothing more to say about it, and she turned back to the readout machine.

"Take care, won't you, Lieutenant?"

I thought to set her right, to tell her that it was just Officer Wright, and then, I realised, with a kinda chill up the spine, that Captain Hughes had come by here and offered me the second-highest post on his ship.

Sure, it was 'just' a Pelter, a fighter with no more than a crew of thirty or so. But it was a start—a *real* start—and for the first time in my FSA service I was gonna have some pretty weighty responsibility on my shoulders.

And, though I wouldn't *ever* have admitted it aloud, I noted to myself that I was a little afraid. Just a little.

Next thing I wondered was just how Doctor Mutely had got wind of the news. Then again, even on a ship of thousands of people, news travels pretty quick. It *was* a closed environment after all. And, of course, she had access to the service records. But even I knew that the bureaucracy of the FSA would never allow for such a quick update, and it made me wonder if she was on some kinda friendly terms with Captain Hughes.

And so, I thanked the good doctor yet again, and unfortunately didn't get so much as a shrug by way of reply, and then I just shucked on out, back to my bunk, and to get in touch with Captain Hughes, to let him know that I was ready to accept his offer.

5

WELL, responsibilities on the Pelter, known by the attractive and catchy P-0993c, were pretty much what I'd expected. Which was to say that it was my job to chew into pretty much everybody. For want of a better term, I was Captain Hughes's eyes and ears on board, though I didn't think much of it till one day when I overheard a pair of crewmembers chewing the shit off in the cafeteria.

I'd just come back down from the bridge, where I'd been off checking over the job some crap-ass engineer had done on recalibrating the laser canons. I'd finally got it all done with and was getting ready to go catch one of my three-times-daily, hour-long naps. Before I'd never had much time at all for naps, never thought that I'd be able to simply slump down in my bunk and catch a wink of sleep.

Guess I'd never accounted for ever doing proper service as a Lieutenant on an FSA ship, because whenever I got half a chance I could lie myself right down and a second later I'd been fast asleep. Total-black, dreamless sleep. And then, an hour later, I'd automatically wake up, if some kinda minor emergency hadn't waked me before then.

And so, that day, just as I was passing by the cafeteria, I heard a pair of officers from on board the *P-0993c* talking. The first one, a guy that I knew straight away, just from his speaking, and someone I wasn't all that fond of, to put it lightly, was going on about the new Lieutenant . . . about *me*.

Well, I was of half a mind to trudge in right then, and to catch them in the middle of that phrase. And, let me tell you, that it's seen as just fine in the FSA for the brass to get their hands dirty on any occasion they deem it needed. In fact, just that day I'd had Captain Hughes, when we'd been having our morning briefing coffee, going on about how all insubordination, no matter how withery or weak it seemed, needed nippin' right in the bud, straight off the bat. Else it might crop up at a much worse time . . . like in the middle of a battle.

And yet, right there in the hall, I knew just what I shoulda done, rushed in there, perhaps smashed a few cups, sent some cutlery a janglin' about the place, and maybe shaken just a bit of sense into that guy.

But I just held back. Didn't seem right to move from my spot. And I listened.

The officer was going on about me, and I knew from what I'd heard off the crew that he was mainly bitter about having been overlooked for the job of Lieutenant on board the *P-0993c*.

You gotta get your politics understood as soon as you possibly can when you enter a new environment.

Anyway, it was when he got to doing this impersonation of me and the captain right there in the cafeteria that really got to me, that made me get all tight with fury inside, made me crunch up my fingers into fists and begin to shake.

The feeling was near-on indescribable, because what I wanted to do was go total crazy and smash shit up, and yet, at the same time, I just stood there, rooted to the spot. And I waited to hear the officers out. To hear just what they had that they couldn't, neither of them, say to my face.

Oh, the officer, he put on a pretty good Arkle accent and, from the seeming of things, he'd picked up that the captain was from there too, or at least that was the joke that got his companion all chucklin' and slappin' at his thigh.

Never before have I felt so thoroughly pissed off. But, at the same time, so frozen in my place, like all this was just existing beyond me. Beyond my consciousness.

I missed out on the end of the conversation, no idea why. Perhaps I'd just slipped into some kinda daze and lost the plot altogether. But I do remember the stirring of the feet, the tinkling of the cups gettin' shoved in the pot cleaner, and then the two officers emerging out into the hall, coming nose to nose with me.

And I just stared on back, those fists down at my sides, pretty much useless, or whatever, and just about a million violent acts crossed my mind.

But I didn't think to do any of them.

Couldn't so much as twitch a muscle.

And then that officer, that bastard he was, he held his fingers up to his forehead and gave me a salute with a grin. "Lieutenant," he said, before he shuffled back off along the corridor, with his crony intact behind him, rustling along like a tame dog at his heels.

Officer Brennant was his name.

And Officer Juklems his companion.

Bright red hair, Brennant had, and a wiggle to his walk.

Juklems's description escapes me, he was just one of those laughing hyenas that so easily drifts into the shadows, their face gettin' all obscure and ever-changing

I just stared on into the corridor behind Officer Brennant, to where he'd disappeared, and feeling the blood boiling away inside me. At that point another series of eventualities struck me, and I thought on going off to the captain, like a schoolmarm, or some such, to tell him just what I'd heard. But I knew that I had to stand up for myself. And I had to fill those Lieutenant's boots or *no one* would respect me.

Above all else, I just couldn't freeze.

Not again.

6

ONE THING that all the thinking doesn't prepare you for when you first think about seeing service on a Pelter is all the inaction. By that I mean just all the downtime, all that time just knocking about the ship not really with anything much of anything to do.

Oh sure, we had a few skirmishes, had to take care of a few rogue ships that came to bothering the mother ship, to buzzing just a little too close for comfort to the *FSA-0100T*. No cannons, or at least nothing more than warning fire.

Funny the sense most people get knocked into them after they've seen a few laser flashes fly out before them.

Aside from those minor showdowns there was really nothing much going on. But one thing all that quiet time did for me was let me get a handle on the crew and, I thought, get them to respect me just a little more.

And so that was how I found it for the longest time, just getting by with very minor things, these straying ships and such. That was till the day when Captain Hughes called me into his quarters and gave me the lowdown.

As I walked that narrow corridor off the main hallway, I listened to my boot steps echoing all about me, and I could smell that harsh metallic scent in the air that I knew to be the liquid related to the ventilation cooling systems.

It was funny since, back on Arkle-4, I never *ever* would've imagined myself to actually get my head around a ship like I had the *P-0993c*. But the thing was that it was pretty much like just another part of me by that time. Like an extra arm or leg.

I'd just shovelled down a cereal cube when I'd got the call, so I was still mushing those little morsels of cereal about the front of my teeth, and tryin' to swallow everything that needed swallowing. But I still had little pieces of cereal stuck between my teeth, and I knew they'd nag away at me till I got them out.

That was funny too, considering that, back on Arkle-4, it'd be a rare day that I'd go take a shower. Most the time there wasn't any water to wash in. I guess that joining up with the FSA had changed my natural habits and feelings more than I'd accounted for.

I pressed my palm flat against the scanner beside the door to Captain Hughes's quarters and the light beneath my skin glowed green, and I listened to the mechanism snick off and the door slide back.

I stepped inside.

—————

Captain Hughes sat over at his holotable, checking over a large 4D render of the surrounding area. I could see the mother ship there, and I could see us too, amongst the rest of the fleet of Pelters. Our ship, the *P-0993c*, was illuminated in a kinda pale green.

Hughes looked up at me and gave me one of his wiry smiles. "Officer Wright, how ya doin' there?"

I still hadn't got over the way that we spoke pure Arkle when we were together, and how different it was to how we spoke in front of the rest of the crew. And by that I knew that Hughes was just as comfortable in my company as I was in his.

He gestured to the seat in front of him at the table, and I took up his offer, and slumped myself down there.

My muscles were aching quite a bit, and my spine felt a sharp tingle run up it. That morning I'd spent a good amount of time in the gym, keeping whatever needed keepin' tight, but also to flush out a great deal of that frustration. See, I'd had another run-in with that Officer Brennant I mentioned before, the one back in the cafeteria, and the best way to get that out my system was to stretch my body to the brink of hell.

Hughes met my eye then wrestled my gaze onto the map sitting before us, the rendered hologram there with us and the space all about us. "Got a distress call this morning, Arkle."

"That so?"

"Uh huh," Hughes replied.

He tapped away at the control panel to the hologram map, his fingers flying over it all, and the map transforming quickly—zooming out to show a longer view of the space about us.

I looked on, seeing that he'd brought a planet into the picture, a solitary planet like the ton of them that you'd find out on the rim of the Fritten System. Right at the edges of the System things get a little dark, and not a little scary, and so that's why there's always a hefty FSA presence in those areas.

Where we were right then.

Now gettin' these distress calls wasn't out the ordinary at all, especially out on the rim of the Fritten. Since there was a combination of mob rule and rebellions springing up just about all over the place out here, there was bound to be some poor soul who decided to send up a message to a passing FSA patrol to come take care of the situation with whoever was the villain of the week.

And this time it turned out that that FSA patrol was us.

Problem, though, as always with this stuff,

was that there simply wasn't enough space for the whole FSA fleet to cover, and jus' as inevitable as playing Whack-a-Mole, soon as we'd taken care of one planet, wrestled the power of the settlement back into some kinda diplomatic shape, and then shuttled off some-place else, the mobsters or rebels would arrive just as quick and shift things back to just how they'd been before.

It was a thankless task, mostly, but these people paid their taxes just like the rest of the Fritten System, and so, as I reckoned it, they deserved just as much protection as we could manage.

Hughes wrinkled his brow as he brought the hologram tighter to the planet up ahead, a real sad-looking place, all out there on its own— at least Arkle-4 has three other planets for company, it isn't just floatin' out there all alone.

"Intelligence has been keepin' a good eye on this place."

"Yeah?" I said.

"Yeah," Hughes said, still not shifting his eyes off the map. "This ain't like those other cases we've been involved with thus far, you know, it's a little more complicated than that."

"How so?"

"Well, thing is that this planet right here, Orkron-1, it's been pretty much plagued by a rebel stronghold for as long as I've known it."

"Sounds standard to me."

Hughes glanced up at me, meeting my eye briefly before looking back down at the holomap. "Command wants us to lead a strike team down there, to go knock out their headquarters. Think that'll knock the stuffing out the rebels for the whole area around here." He looked up again, this time lingering a little longer on my eye. "This could be a great step forward for us, Arkle, could be that we liberate this whole area from the clutches of the rebels."

"Sounds good to me."

"Yeah," he said, turning back to the holomap. "It does that."

"So what's the plan?"

Hughes swallowed hard, and I watched his Adam's apple bob in his throat. I caught another whiff of that cooling liquid from the ventilation ducts and only then I realised that I was sweatin' real hard. I mean, damn, my whole uniform was almost totally plastered in sweat. And that cereal I spoke about—the little grains stuck in my teeth?—they were just flat pissing me right off now, and I'd a done anything for a healthy swig of mouthwash.

Not the time nor the place for that, though.

Just a little way off, back beyond Hughes's shut door, I could hear the stomping of boots through the corridor, and I knew that before I'd even got into the captain's quarters, that he'd already given the order to the bridge to get geared up.

For us to prepare to go to war.

Hughes stared long and hard at me. "We got ourselves fitted with one of these new-fangled cloakers last night. Had the maintenance boys from the mother ship fitting them."

"Thought there was a bunch of clanking and sparking last night, guess that's my explanation."

Hughes smiled briefly, but that smile just as quick slipped off his lips. "Yeah, they got us fitted with the cloakers just fine."

After that Hughes just seemed to drift off into some daze and, when I looked into his eyes, I could see that he was floatin' off, just miles away. I thought about snapping my fingers, bringing him back with a wry smile like I was a hypnotist or some such.

When I looked back to the holomap I saw that a region on the planet had now been marked out in a neon-red glow, with a wispy floating letter A beside it, and I knew just what that meant without having to ask.

Right there, on the holomap, that was our target.

Seeing that Hughes was just doin' some thinking of his own and guessing he wanted to be left alone right there and then, I got up off my chair, gave the captain his salute, and made for the door.

Just as I got ready to punch the release on the locking system, he spoke.

"Arkle?"

"Sir?"

Another long and pregnant pause, and I could hear just about all the ticking going on in the ship, all those tiny little parts that kept us flying through space so quick, the pumping of those liquids and gases that kept us alive out here in this great big vacuum.

"You just get everything checked out, 'kay?"

"Yes, sir," I said, and then slapped the locking system and the door slid open.

I shifted out into the corridor, and away from the captain's quarters, ready to get everyone ready for the assault.

7

WE GOT THE CONFIRMATION CALL round dawn the next day and, just like Captain Hughes had wanted, I had the crew all ready for the raid. The plan was real simple. Jet us in there, stick on our cloakers, then drift right down to the centre of the rebel base and drop the thermonuke right on their heads.

That'd take care of them.

Way that I got the info, from what was re-laid to me by the good lady in charge of our navigational systems, was that this rebel base was placed right out in the centre of this tangled, jungle mess on the planet.

Thousands of klicks from any of the official settlements on Orkron-1.

From what I saw of the terrain maps, I just saw a bunch of shitty-looking bogs, just all puffing out farty gases into the atmosphere. Not that I'm one to talk since my home planet is Arkle-4, but there you go, that was just what entered my mind at the time.

Nah, this would be a perfect sweep, and it would set all the good people of Orkron-1, all those mothers and children and the good fathers free from these blood-sucking rebels on their planet, who were snaffling up their food and, no doubt, romancing daughters.

That was the thing with rebels that I've never quite understood, never really been able to set apart in much of a way from mob rule. And it's that, once they get going, whatever political or ideals they started off a fightin' for, that pretty much just gets lost out of the chute once they realise they can use those laser blasters of theirs to live out their version of paradise.

So I didn't stop to think for one minute about that thermonuke we were packing on board, and the damage it would do to them.

The hundreds—thousands?—of rebels it would take out with its punch.

I *knew*, just as sure as I'd grown up on Arkle-4 with those mobsters thumbing just about everything down they could, that the eradication of these foul parasites would be the best thing that happened in any of their lives.

Which was to say nothing about how it would help out with the other planets these rebels were holdin' in their sway, oppressing just so they'd feel like great *big* men . . . and women too, because those rebel women can be just as bad.

If truth be told, this was just what I'd signed up for the FSA for.

Oh fine, sure the whole attraction of flying on a spaceship—gettin' away from Arkle-4—had been mighty powerful too.

But, deep down, I knew that I wanted to set people free and, I guess, I once harboured the wish of going back to Arkle-4 and doin' just the same.

———

I stood up on the bridge in my normal place, at

the left-hand side of the captain's chair, meanwhile Captain Hughes sat with his back rigid there, looking over all the various holopanels stretched out before him—the seemingly endless maps, and dials, and meters and all the like.

I also noted that Officer Brennant was off in his chair, doing his job to keep the engineering deck under control. I just hoped that he'd be a professional about it and put whatever he didn't like about me and the captain to one side for the fate of the mission.

Because when you're packing a thermonuke all sorts of shit can go down. The annals of FSA history is littered with Pelters packing thermonukes and then gettin' themselves into a whole multitude of troubles.

And I had very little interest of *my* entry in those same annals going anything along those lines.

We were bringing her in quick, just as we'd got the orders to do so, and I was keepin' an eye on everything that Captain Hughes couldn't. And I was also tapping the pulse of the room, tryin' to get a handle on just how everyone was feeling up there on the bridge.

It was my job to know if someone was gonna freak out at any point, or have some part of their job slip their mind. That was what I'd been taught on all those training courses I'd taken over the several months since I'd been appointed Lieutenant to Captain Hughes.

And I was keeping an especially close eye on Brennant. Though I didn't really want to admit as much to myself, I was looking for some solid reason to get him chucked from the Pelter. I guess I could've justified it in saying he could wreck morale on board, but I wanted something meatier, something that'd get him off for good, and wouldn't be liable to being discussed on some council board somewhere on the mother ship.

We were coming up close on the entry to Orkron-1 and I could already feel the shudder as the Pelter began to make contact with the flimsy atmosphere surrounding the place. I glanced over to the captain, got the nod, and then gave the order for everyone to take their seats for the impending impact.

Then I strapped myself in and readied myself for the bumpy ride.

I caught the juddering hard, and I felt my teeth gnashing away, feeling almost like the enamel was gettin' all chipped off as we entered the atmosphere. I could also feel the shift of the thrusters, gettin' adjusted to being planetside, and I heard a new *hum*, one that seemed to penetrate the whole Pelter, and drive right through my bones.

And I knew that was the sensation of the cloakers kickin' into gear, so that we would stay out of sight on the systems down below, so the rebels would never see us comin'.

I shifted over to take a look at the navigational systems, and to our current location. We were a good five minutes from the target, from the drop-off point.

I glanced over to the other side of the bridge and saw the thermonuke being prepped by proxy by the officer seated over there. The thermonuke itself was way down in the belly of the Pelter. I saw the proxy the officer was workin' on was sittin' on Standby mode, ready for the order to be set off. If there was a spark, or something went wrong right then, it

wouldn't just have blown us right out of the sky
. . . it would've blown us into tiny little bits, and
then those tiny little bits into tinier bits still.

I guess I was sweatin' just a little more
then, and I could feel my heart jigging up into
my throat all the more, and the blood a pumpin'
all the harder round my veins. I gripped the
armrests tight and knew that our success just
depended on us doin' all our jobs right. And
that we should just drift in, cloakers engaged,
drop out payload and be long gone before the
thermonuke pounded out a new crater in the
face of Orkron-1.

I was watchin' the clock tickin' down, it'd
got to be about two and a half minutes before
we'd reach the drop-off point when I noticed
the flashin' on the navigational screen. Seemingly hundreds of little flashing dots.

Ships.

Rebel Ships.

And they had us all surrounded.

8

FIRST THING that struck my mind was wild and weary confusion. Next up, when the tiny fragment of my logical brain thought to kick in, I realised that it must be a fleet of these rebel ships, of these guys swarming the air of Orkron-1. And then I reasoned that, most likely, it was a training exercise. That these ships just happened to be out here, cropping up on our navigational screens, pulsing about, coming in our direction.

I looked away from the open-mouthed officer at the navigational screens and glanced over to the captain, letting him know what'd just popped through my head.

But, before Captain Hughes got even the

faintest chance to respond to me, he'd already shifted right off to staring at the real-time screens hitting us from the space opening out before us, to exactly where our Pelter was headed.

And those rebel ships were forming up on our hull, getting into attack formation. There was almost no time for me to bark out an order to Brennant, to demand he check on the cloakers, that he make sure they were fully functioning.

But either he just sat there plain stunned or he didn't hear me before the first of the rapping laser fire pounded against the side of the Pelter.

———

By that time, I saw just what was happening and, almost like a waking dream, I watched things unfold before my eyes, saw just what had to be done. And I reeled off the order, without so much as consulting Captain Hughes, for us to shift all power off the cloakers —which were draining our energy cells at a rate of knots—and to throw everything we had into the shields.

These rebel ships could see us just fine anyhow, so we didn't need the cloakers.

Already I could see the damage reports reeling in, in their neon-green lettering, just rolling their way up the screen, telling us that this or that thruster was burned out, or that our stabilisers were thrown off balance . . . that they needed to be *recalibrated*.

If ever there was a time for recalibration it certainly wasn't then.

What we needed right then was total and complete, fast-moving action.

Once the shields were up things got a sight better. At least the proximity alarms thought to give us just a little break, just for a few seconds for those wails to flush out of my hearing and sink a little further into the gooey mass of my brain.

The rebel ships just kept coming, wave upon wave, unrelenting, pounding us with their laser cannons. And I felt every rock and bump as they flashed our shields all round us. When I glanced over at the navigational screen to my side I saw that they were closing a perimeter round us, that they were making an effort to block our escape.

And then I knew just what had to be done if we were to have any chance of preserving the souls of those on board the Pelter.

I yammered on at Captain Hughes, who remained in his chair, staring at the screens as they pounded out reel after reel of more information. I knew that he wasn't stunned, that he wasn't overwhelmed by all this, I knew that the fact of the thing was that he was thinking, and he knew that there wasn't anything so deadly as a mistimed or ill-judged command.

He trusted me enough to do the grunt command work, to keep us sailing just fine in the middle of this almighty shitstorm we found ourselves right in the centre of. And it took just about all my capacities to get across the thing about the thermonuke, that we needed to shut the fucking thing off before these rebel ships penetrated our shields.

Else it would mean all our lives.

As I sat there, staring at the captain's face in profile, I knew just what conflicts were flying through his mind, between those jutting-out ears, and I knew that he was thinking of the oath all of us took at one point or another, that he was wonderin' whether this was one of those times when we *had* to put our lives on the line to take out the rebels.

I caught his voice, thick and raspy, as he spoke. "Yeah," he said, "you shut that thing off, fast as you can." Then he turned straighter on to me. "Quick. It's gotta be done."

9

QUICK AS THAT, I gave the order. I turned in my seat and demanded that the thermonuke get switched to Disarmed as fast as possible. The officer's voice was almost totally stripped away from the shrieking of the reverse thrusters, of the pounding of those laser cannons up against the ship's hide, but I still made it out.

Or, at least, I caught the upshot of the thing.

The remote control proxy on the thermonuke was set to Standby, and so if—*when*—those piled-up rebel ships managed to penetrate the shields, any stray spark, let alone a direct hit from a laser cannon, would set that thing off.

And it'd make the rebels just as dead as us.

Not that they had any way of knowing just what our intentions were, let alone what we had on board.

I sat there in my chair, feeling my guts fizz and my mind draw blank after blank after blank. But I knew just what needed doin' and I was just cheating myself, cheating *all* of us, not to get it done.

And so, feeling the whole ship, a whole assortment of fields tugging at me, I whipped off my seatbelt and leaped up out of my seat.

Almost immediately, I felt the soles of my boots slip on the floor, and my whole body seem to almost fly away from me. Next thing I knew, I was having the air squeezed out of me as I lay pressed up against the wall of the bridge.

I was winded, frantically trying to strip breaths from the base of my lungs, and yet they came hard and insufficient, when they came at all.

Then I felt steady hands on me, helping me out of my predicament, tugging me loose from the forces all pinning me there. And soon enough I was back on my feet. The ship had stabilised and we were back shooting on a horizontal trajectory.

When I glanced round to see who'd helped me up, I saw the face of Officer Brennant, a firm smile pressed on his lips, as he got himself back into his seat, and strapped himself back in.

As I rushed off the bridge I caught the words mouthed on his lips.

'Good luck.'

———

I felt my pulse hammering away at my temples and I could taste blood in my mouth. All round my mouth, in fact. And I had no desire to look down at myself either because I was sure I'd find blood soaking the whole front of my uniform.

Patching up could come later, first off I had to have a go at saving us all from this thermonuke that was wired to blow at any second right about now.

I lurched from side to side with the movements of the ship, as the thrusters roughly compensated for the stabilisers being well busted. I knew that Captain Hughes, back on the bridge, was doin' all he could to give me a smooth ride out to the back of the Pelter, but there was only so much he could do considering that we were under heavy, *heavy* rebel fire.

Whatever he could do, I appreciated it.

Soon enough, and not without another fair few knocks against the steel walls, I got myself into the maintenance unit, and I caught sight of the engineers all around me. All of them were strapped into their seats of course. And they looked at me with wild eyes as I pounded past them, still bouncing off the walls whenever the ship jerked from one side to another. They thought I was crazy, and they mighta been right.

But sometimes—just *sometimes*—crazy saves the day just fine.

I lashed my way along the tight corridors, taking care not to snag too many wires as I bundled past. I knew that if I was to break something then it'd be me that'd have to fix the thing, and me and fixin', for the longest time now, have never gone together.

I picked out the entrance to the weapons deck, where the thermonuke was sitting all primed, on its perch, ready to be dropped wherever it was that it needed droppin', and I bundled my way inside, the security scanner just blinking its green light at my palm, givin' me no gyp on my way through, as if it understood the predicament we all found ourselves in.

———

On the weapons deck, the thermonuke was hard to miss. Why, it sat there right in the middle of the floor, set atop its perch, above those folding bay doors, looking all prim and ready for its jump.

I wondered, just for a second, whether I could manually operate the doors, if I could— just *maybe*—set the thing to drop right from here, right plumb down on top of the rebel headquarters.

But that was a dumb thought since I knew there was really no telling just where we were at that moment in time, just where that thermonuke would drop.

Why, we mighta been thrown off course so hard, that we were right above one of those settlements right about now . . . above a school as far as I knew.

No, the thermonuke needed deactivating and it needed doin' now. Else it was gonna make one hell of a *pop* when we got ourselves shot up.

I stumbled over the deck, and over to the nuke, sitting there on its perch. I worked quickly, drawing again on my training to become a Lieutenant, my hands working fast through the screens, whipping through them and bringing up the options available:

Deactivate. Standby. Arm.

My fingers were shaking hard and my heart goin' so fast that my blood going to my brain seemed like an afterthought. And as the ship bucked up and down as it tried to find some form of equilibrium, I was certain that I was gonna punch the wrong option by mistake.

But, for one sacred, still moment, I managed to get my finger to do just what I wanted from it. I got it to hold still and to punch the Standby option.

The screen on the thermonuke changed

from its sickly tangerine colour, to a neutral, passive blue. And I knew that I'd succeeded. That I'd saved us all from a sticky, pounding, high-energy death.

The rebels too.

Though I guessed that in the condition we were in, coupled with the pounding we were taking from their cannons, it all added up to us just tryin' to get out of this thing alive right now.

The rest could wait.

————

It was a rocky trek back up to the bridge, but I made it just fine. In fact, when I got back in there I could almost feel the adrenalin eking its way back out of my bloodstream, letting me be for once. And it seemed like right there, up on the bridge, that everything was totally still, everyone seemingly mesmerised.

And then, catching up with my senses, I saw just why that was.

Right up ahead of us, facing down with the hull of our Pelter, there was a big, *mean* ship. One of the rebel ships.

And it had one of those dirty, great big cannons to go with its enormous size.

That, I guess, was the moment when I knew for certain that we were all done for. Even before I saw the first flash of its gigantic cannon, firing off rounds right for us.

10

THE LASER BLASTS sent shocks skittering all over the shields surrounding the Pelter. My mind got all numb and the Pelter lurched over to the left, and then the right. Next thing I knew we were plummeting down, the whole front of the ship totally filled with the dark-green foliage all spread out below.

I grabbed a hold of some chair and managed to cling on as we swilled downwards, the ground coming up faster at us with each passing second. My mouth tasted all salty and I could smell the burned-out mechanical systems, or whatever it was that was a burnin'.

I caught sight of the officer sitting at the ship controls, trying to get a hold of the descent, and saw that, little by little, the nose of the Pelter was anglin' its way upwards. I even saw a little glimpse of the purple-black sky at the top of the screen before it slipped away again.

All the thrusters screeched out and although the ship had levelled out again, shootin' back along horizontal, it was still banking unpredictably, and I had to take extreme care not to end up sprawled against some wall or other.

I clambered my way along the floor of the bridge and somehow managed to drag myself up into my chair, where I propped myself up and took in the screens bearing down on us.

The readings spiralled out of control, constantly ticking along, adding more and more problems to ones we'd already got. But my eyes soon searched through those heaps of damage readouts and rested on the one that I knew, to us, was the most important of all.

The afterburners. The engines that'd get us back out of the atmosphere, and back out into space, on the way back to the mother ship.

Captain Hughes spoke quick and his voice was uneven, and he kept on breaking into that thick Arkle accent of his even though all his crew were spread around him. I guess when you get to panickin', get to the point where you're about to die, that's where you just don't care what anyone thinks of you no more.

"Arkle, we've sent a distress signal back at the *FSA-0100T*."

"They respond?" I said, amazed I managed to get any words out at all, because, by now, the Pelter was skirting the tops of the forest canopy, and I watched the leaves and branches crushed beneath the Pelter's belly as we barrelled on.

Hughes got all bug-eyed. "They can't Arkle. Think it's a trap. The rebels knew we were comin', saw right through . . . right through the cloaker, and so there's no tellin' jus' what they might have in store for us."

"So we're on our own?" I said, thinking about the afterburners being, well, all burned-out, and knowing already that my assumption was correct.

Hughes nodded anyway.

I sat back in my chair and watched the

navigating officers go at it, piloting the ship to the best of their ability, swinging it about and keeping it just out of the way of the larger branches of the canopy.

I clenched my teeth as we rocked our way over the branches, as the branches kept on tickling the Pelter's belly as it went, and I almost convinced myself I could hear those branches scatchin' away at the paintwork, but I knew it was impossible over the *squeal* of the thrusters and the alarms all bawling out.

My heart tickled the base of my throat and I could feel my hands gettin' all clammy. Right about then I dug my fingernails in deep into the arms of my chair, feeling the material flex and wane just a little under my touch. And I knew, whatever happened now, that was where I was gonna stay. No chance anyone was gonna get me out of that chair with anythin' less than a crowbar.

And just as that daze rolled down me, Hughes looked to me and said, "Arkle, there's only one way of us getting' out of this mess, you know that, right?"

The thrusters and alarms got even louder,

just for a moment, and they seemed to get so hard, so thick in the air, that they could pound against my skull, turn my brain into putty all over again.

11

FOR SOME REASON my mind shot me back off to Arkle-4. Back to my home planet. And I saw myself walking back down my old hallway, back to our apartment there. I could hear the blabbing coming from the entertainment units beyond the closed doors, and could smell the wax that buffed the floors to a heady shine. And all along I had that taste of Snarple Crank at the back of my mouth, and I knew pretty much what was going on. That I'd just come home from school, or some such.

As I got closer to the door of my apartment, I could feel the tang of the Snarple Crank getting almost too tough to handle, make my stomach buck and rumble. I walked on a little quicker, a touch harder, hearing my footsteps echoing about the hallway. I caught sight of our door, a pale-blue colour with dozens and dozens of stains just blasted all over it.

The door was also made of steel, and cold, and built to keep stuff out, and all. To keep whatever stuff we had in our apartment safe from any passing lowlife wantin' to burgle what little we had.

For some reason I felt torn about gettin' back home. On the one hand I was glad, truly glad about it since I hated school, and I liked my bedroom pretty well. And then there was the matter of all that Snarple Crank rolling about my system, and I needed to get to our toilet . . . just as soon as I could.

So, I was out there in the hall, and before I knew it, before I could put my finger on just what seemed weird about the whole deal, I reached out and set my hand up against the scanner.

That green glow flushed up against my palm, and I felt the slightly warm tickle of those systems all working to identify who I was, and whether or not to let me into the place.

Before I knew it, the steel door was rollin'

back on itself, rollin' right back into the wall, and out of sight, laying out the apartment right before me, all ready for me to step into.

I held back, felt my breath hitch in my throat just a sec, and then I stumbled forwards into the apartment.

———

Well, I was pretty much headed for the toilet, making my way through the hallway that always seemed to be rollin' with tingling, chilly draughts, when I overheard some voices mutterin'. That caught me off guard somewhat seein' as no one shoulda been home that time, and that my little bro was still off back at school doing time for some teacher or other, for showin' up late or not doing his homework, or whatever. And Mum and Dad, well, they shoulda been at work, or so I thought.

. . . Because right then and there was when I heard them speaking, I heard my mum and dad back home, speaking in low voices in the sitting room, what was the sitting room and their bedroom. Just as I was about to stamp off to say hi to them, I heard another, unfamiliar voice, and I just stopped right where I was.

Couldn't go no further.

And I just stood there, out in the hallway and listened on in.

My mum and dad, they were just speakin' with this guy, this guy with this slimy-as-guts voice who kept on coughing and spittin'. I waited them out, tried to hear just what they was saying, but I had no chance at that at all. And so I tried to sneak on by, to get past the doorway, and to the toilet at the end of the hall.

Just as I passed by the doorway, without even lookin', I could feel my parents' eyes roll onto me. And then my mum, she said, "Arkle? You home from school?"

Slowly, I turned my head and looked to them, to the room that served as their sitting room, and their bedroom, and then I looked to the man in the raggedy, sweeping leather jacket, and the toothpick physique. He had scrappy grey whiskers, and bunched-up, rosy-red cheeks. I recognised him, 'course I recognised him, but the real matter was just *who* he was . . . and who he worked for.

The man was a dealer, a guy who I'd seen

hanging 'bout the place for years, probably ever since I could get to recognising stuff. And I always knew that he was Bad News, and that my mum and dad themselves was always warning me to take care round him.

His name was Ernest Harry and he worked for Big Jo, the biggest mob man in our area.

Now, though, I was shocked, just didn't understand what this man was doin' here in our apartment. And then I saw the credits, all stacked up on the half-smashed-up coffee table, and I knew just what was goin' on.

Money troubles.

It had to be.

Even when I was just a kid I knew what 'money troubles' meant. And though I was just a kid I knew what damage it could do . . . how desperate Mum and Dad musta been . . . to get involved with someone like Ernest Harry.

Mum, she just smiled at me, and made her way over, while Dad just kept up his conversation with Ernest Harry, and how Dad kept on glancin' back to that pile of credits on the coffee table.

And I just kept quiet, *so* still, not daring to move a muscle unless I did somethin' wrong, and, maybe in my child's mind, I thought that Ernest Harry might come for me . . . or somethin' like that.

Somethin' wild like that.

That weren't the last time I saw Ernest Harry in our apartment or nothin' either, and I soon worked out that both Mum and Dad had got themselves fired from the munitions factory nearby where they both worked—where they'd *met*—and that they needed the money to keep things tickin' along for me and my bro.

Nothing ever seemed much to go wrong with the arrangement, but I couldn't help thinkin', from then on, that me and my bro, that we were some kind of *burden*. I guess, when those men from the FSA, when they came by and they offered me something else, a chance to get off Arkle at seventeen years old, and to get off my parents' backs, then I . . . well, I mighta resisted a while or so, but I soon knew just what was best for my family.

They could manage much better with just my bro with them.

And, ever since I'd joined up the FSA, I'd never once gone back home, never once gone back *there*. And, after four solid years of service, and now sitting on my twenty-first birthday, I wondered if I ever would get back there.

Because, goodness knows, there was nothin' there for me back on Arkle-4.

12

"ARKLE! ARKLE!"

Captain Hughes's voice came at me like words from underwater. My whole brain felt like damp cotton wool, and I was gripping the armrests of my chair so hard now that a few of my fingernails had split. The sweat rolled down my forehead in constant rivulets, and the shakes had me in their grasp.

I managed to jerk my head round to take in Captain Hughes, who was half out of his chair, eyes bulging almost out their sockets. He gave me a kinda delirious smile then said, "Good, thought I'd lost ya then, Arkle."

When I looked round properly, I could only see the foliage below, seeming to just about swarm right below us, almost like it might swallow us up whole. Then my eyes flushed over to the navigational screens, and I saw that great big blob—the rebel's huge ship—and I realised it was gaining on us, surely preparing for its last, great strike.

Captain Hughes was sweatin' hard and I realised just then that about half the medical bay were on the bridge, checking over bloody heads and such, and that while the ship was just about staggering along as soon as the mother ship hit us with those cannons again we'd be finished.

And right then I knew just what Captain Hughes was gonna say. Maybe, thinking back on it now, I was actually mouthing along with his words. Or maybe it's something to do with shock, you know.

That was when I noticed Captain Hughes had a rip in his trouser leg, that something had struck him during the whole chaos of this raid on Orkron-1. Maybe it'd been a bit of technocrap fallin' from the roof or something, all I knew was that the captain was breathing hard and sweatin' whole buckets, and it all fell to me now.

I had to take action.

"Arkle," he started, already going into just what I knew he was gonna say. "Communications to engineering deck are down. Only way's you're gonna save us now's if you can get down to them, tell them just what they've gotta do. The afterburners gotta be back online, gotta get them jiggin' again. That's the only chance we've got of blasting back off into space—gettin' ourselves out of this well pissed-up mess, got it?"

I did get it, but, at the same time, I felt like my whole body was rigid as a board, and I simply knew that even if I'd shouted at my legs they never would've shifted out from beneath me. I couldn't even shout, though. All I could think to do was watch the foliage continue to fill the screen before us, seem to swallow up the whole of my damn vision, and I got all nauseous, and my brain got all skittered as I thought about what was gonna happen to us.

What a disaster we'd got ourselves set up for.

"Arkle!" Captain Hughes said again, this time with a little more steel in his voice, and when I cast a glance over him I saw that his brows were knitted and he had a bunch of wrinkles inset in his forehead. "That's an order. Get the hell down there and get those afterburners fixed right this instant!"

Now, I mighta come into the FSA with somethin' of a reputation as a tearaway. Oh, I'd drink and swear and talk back and such, but the one problem I never had was insubordination, I knew as good as my left foot that if someone barked something at me, I was to jump to it right away.

Only now I couldn't. I simply couldn't. I was just all froze up.

"Officer Wright!" Captain Hughes repeated. "Jump to it!"

But my fingernails just kept up their vice-like grip on the arms of my chair and I knew there'd be no shifting them.

No shifting them at all.

When I looked back at him, with what I guessed was that blank stare of mine, those slightly parted lips, I could see the surprise washing over his face. That this man, the one that he'd selected, thought to be the hardest of the hard—the officer who'd gone and survived twice as long as anyone else down in the deserts of Asfarth-14, was freezing up on him now, and with it killing all hope of getting out of this blithe mess.

Captain Hughes gave me a kinda half-sneer and I thought he was readying to launch into some tirade of insults, to give me a proper barking at. But, instead, he shifted round in his seat, grimacing from whatever injury he had to his leg, and he fixed Officer Brennant in his stare.

He gave him the same order he'd given me and Officer Brennant, currently helping out Officer Juklems who'd got himself a nasty gash to his head, leaped right up from his spot, and beat it off the bridge and down the corridor without question.

Next off, and I'll always remember this —*always*—to my dying day, I caught that frostiest of frosty glares off of Captain Hughes.

And I knew then, just as I know as well now, that I deserved every last flinch of the eyelid of that glare, every snarl of the lip, and each tautening of the muscles in his neck.

When the laser blasters came, when they rained down on us, blowing right through our shields, and finally sending a distinct and echoing *crack* through the whole of the Pelter, I caught Captain Hughes's face embossed on the backs of my eyelids as I sealed them tight and clung on tight to the worn-off material of the arms of my chair

. . . like a fucking baby snatching up the hem of its quilt while it's mewling and bawling in its mother's arms.

13

E VERY LAST ALARM in the ship just
seemed to rip and roar through my skull.
My teeth chattered together and I bit my
tongue at least a dozen or more times. And I
tasted the blood welling up in my mouth,
lolling over everything. The metallic smell
crawled up my nostrils and amped up those
waves of nausea pumpin' through me.

The pit of my stomach seemed to
completely fall away as the ship plummeted
down. And I could hear the screaming—the
human screamin'—competing with the ship's
alarms and the failing thrusters and the flashin'
of the shields outside of us, now beaten for once
and for all.

My hearing dipped in and out, and my consciousness came and went. It was kinda like watching everything happen out in a dream. And, in the same way, it was like none of this would ever hurt me, like it would never actually cause me any harm.

But that all changed when I heard the *scratches* and *creaks* as we fell down through the branches of the forest, the branches way too weak to support the weight of the ship, on our way to rushing right to the floor of the forest.

I remember, right at the last moment, opening up my eyes and looking out, feeling like my eyeballs were a pair of peeled eggs floatin' about in one of my mum's homemade soups, the ones that she'd cobbled together from the money she got off Ernest Harry.

All I saw was brown mulch, all I remember before the one single, almighty, explosion as we hit.

————

My ears just throbbed on along, and a great and immutable ringin' hailed through my brain. I was just about still conscious, and I could hear the alarms goin' off somewhere in the back of my mind, and I could hear the *snick* and *snaggle* of flames springing up here and there . . . and the silent and gentle swarm of the smoke pumping out from every crevice.

Almost right away I got to coughing my lungs up, and I could hardly stop once I'd started. I just kept coughin', over and over again, feeling my insides grow raw.

I felt weird, my neck ached and my muscles felt raw. And then I realised that I was sittin', still buckled into my chair, on an angle, and danglin' out onto the now-slanted bridge.

For a few seconds I just sat slumped there knowing that this was the end. That my once promising career in the FSA was well and truly comin' to an end. And what a way to end it.

Because I knew, even if no one else would, that I had freaked out when the captain had most needed me. I'd got the coward's desease and just clear locked up near enough every bone, muscle and nerve in my body. I wouldn't make no good soldier.

Not anymore.

My senses snapped back to me, one by one, but that ringin' in my ears didn't let up at all.

When I tried to shift myself in my chair I got a snaking pain slithering up my spine, and a red flash across my vision for my trouble. But I told myself I had to get moving, else I would surely die.

There was one thing I could do now, somethin' that *might* at least go some way to recompensing just what I'd done—or *failed* to do—and that was to help get out as many of my fellow crewmembers as I possibly could.

To save whoever I could possibly save.

And so I shucked off my belt, and then immediately fell a metre or so, clattering my head up against some malfunctioning and shrieking unit or other and then, finding my bearings once more, I thrust myself up and looked about me.

Some of the people were comin' round, rubbing their sore heads, their eyes all dancing 'bout their sockets like they'd just woken up from being knocked down in a bar fight. Though what'd just happened was much worse than any bar fight.

The first thought that skittered across my mind, when I'd got myself upright, my body still throbbing with shock, and my skull still beating with that ringin', was to locate the captain. And I did that right away.

The captain remained in his chair, in the chair beside the one I'd just slipped out of. His head was lolled to one side, and his lips slightly parted. I rushed to him, clambering my way up debris to reach him, and I snatched a hold of his wrist and checked his pulse.

Nothing. Nothing at all.

I waited a second, another second, and then maybe five more.

But there was no pulse.

My whole body seemed to blaze with heat, and then I noted a flame that'd burst right through the wall of the bridge, and that people, the officers, were hurriedly tryin' to get away from it . . . or at least the ones that were movin' were.

I seemed to make peace with Captain Hughes being dead pretty fast, all things considered, though I guess it was most likely due to the situation, and that I was just acting on my gut, knowing that anything less than that could easily get me killed here.

And so my next thought was for Officer Brennant, the man who'd gone in my place to go and sort out the problems with the after-burners. At least I could save the man who'd had to step into my shoes . . . the man who *should*, by all rights, have taken the spot of Lieutenant, if it hadn't been for Captain Hughes's misplaced judgement.

So I rushed off the bridge, leaving all those clambering officers behind, and I rushed my way along the corridor, in pursuit of where I knew Officer Brennant to have gone.

14

SALLOW EMERGENCY LIGHTS illuminated the ship now. Smoke smothered the whole of the corridor, seeming to pour out of just about everywhere. I brought my uniform collar up over my nose and mouth, and breathed through it, taking it easy, for the first time in the whole raid actually feeling something of confidence, of calm, descending right over me. And I picked my way through the diagonally-angled corridor, through the broken pieces of technocrap, and remained focussed on my destination.

When I reached the door to the engineering deck, the security panel had got all busted in from the impact, and the door was stuck half-open, its mechanism buzzin' on and on endlessly. I wheedled my way in through the gap, breathing in hard, glad that I'd not put back on all the weight I'd been carrying before my training exercise down on Asfarth-14.

Once inside the engineering bay, I glanced about me, realising how different it all looked to how it had been just an hour or so ago, when I'd first come down here to see to disarming the thermonuke. That seemed a long time ago now and I reminded myself that if I hadn't seen to disarming it then our ship would've been nothing more than a smoking crater right at that moment.

At least I'd done one thing right.

But there was still so much work to be done.

I prowled through the mounted stacks of equipment and the shattered screens, and I peered into the gloom and the lingering smoke about the place trying to find some point of reference, just somethin' that mighta been familiar.

The afterburner controls, I knew, when I got my bearings, was a little further along, deeper into the engineering bay, and so I pushed myself forwards, trying my best not to drink any more smoke than I had to.

And then, up ahead, I saw him.

Even in the sallow light his red hair shone out, and I recognised him right away.

Officer Brennant.

———

I shuffled on through the debris, like I was back among those damn sand dunes, constantly sinking, that sand always draggin' me down. And I could see him there, that he was bleeding from his temple, that somethin' had struck him. But then I saw the whites of his eyes, and his yawning mouth, and I knew that he was conscious.

That he could still be saved.

I felt a kinda sharp lightness rush right through me . . . just this almost indescribable sensation of ecstasy rushing and churning through every one of my veins, and I caught onto that feeling and used it to push myself forwards, to go to his aid.

Though he was lookin' about and such, he couldn't understand my voice when I said his name, and even less when he ogled my face. I guess that bump to the head had really shook him up somethin' bad and I thought to myself at the time, by all rights, that it shoulda been me lying there with the bumped head.

And I'd have made peace with the fact that no one was a comin' to save me. I'd have made peace with death, known that I'd done my duty.

But now, the way things were, the way the cards had been dealt, it meant that my duty right at that moment in time was to save Officer Brennant, to go some way to makin' amends for the situation *I* had left him in.

I was also glad for those muscles of mine, of all the gym work I'd been puttin' in over the past few weeks, and I grabbed a hold of him beneath the armpits and I lugged him over the engineering deck, and back out towards the corridor.

I knew our only hope was Escape Hatch C, just a little way along from here, so I lugged him along, back through the engineering bay, and back out to the corridor.

Every couple of seconds now I heard a *pop* or *fizzle* of some electrical circuit burning itself out, or a cry from some crewmember. But I knew that I just had to keep on goin' along, because I could only carry one person at a time.

And my very first duty was to get Officer Brennant out of there.

Back out in the corridor, the smoke made a good job of just about smothering out the emergency lighting, and it was all I could do to squint through it to make out the hatch above us, and the ladder which ran alongside it.

Because of the angle the ship had crashed in, the ladder was almost on the horizontal so, with Brennant just about conscious enough to follow my directions, to get those lubbering feet of his onto the rungs, we clambered our way up, me behind him making sure he couldn't fall back.

And all the time the smoke came in, buffeting me from both sides, now worming its way through the makeshift nose and mouth covering of the collar of my uniform. But I pushed myself on, telling myself that I still had more people to save, even after I got Brennant back outside.

We reached the top of the ladder and I

shouted out to Brennant. "Shove it! Shove it up!"

But Brennant just seemed all dazed, and I noticed the blood runnin' thicker now down his face, and growing all slick and matted in the sallow light.

Somehow, I gritted my teeth and then reached past him and slammed the escape hatch with the butt of my palm.

The hatch burst open spillin' purple-tinted light in from the outside. The light was so bright that for a few seconds it was dazzling to me. After all that time on spaceships, dealing with artificial lighting, I'd got all accustomed to not having to deal with something so bright.

Brennant remained up there, clinging to the rungs, and seeming not to know what to do next. And then I called up to him, motioned for him to clamber on out, and he finally got the idea.

I followed him up and we emerged out there on the shell of the Pelter, staring down at the forest floor about five or six metres down. It looked soft enough, so I grabbed a hold of a scrap of Brennant's uniform and then pulled us both down.

As I landed on the ground, which turned out even softer than I'd imagined, I bent my knees, and watched Brennant do the same.

My heart ticked on all the harder, and my brain commanded me to keep on movin', to get Brennant out of trouble before I had to go back into the ship to get more people out.

I dragged him through a bunch of thickets of strange, cream-coloured plants that mighta smelled strongly, but in this situation they just stank of spaceship fuel and smoke. Rather than chokin' me, like it had back in the ship, now that same stench drove me forwards, forced me into action.

I picked out a nice-enough lookin' rock and then slumped Brennant down there, where he sat himself up. I looked over him, my eyes surely all glazed over, and wide, and bright. He looked a little dazed but I could see he'd be just fine sittin' over there.

So, with Brennant all safe and stuff, I shifted back out through the foliage, back in the direction of the Pelter.

Just as I got within about a hundred metres from it, and was readying myself to surge forwards, to go sprintin' back for Escape Hatch

C, I was just in time to hear the *fizzle* of the flames reach a fever pitch and, with a welling and slowly enveloping *whomp*, to see the ship burst into a roaring inferno.

And I had enough sense knocked into me at that point to think to throw myself down onto the earth, and the hold my hands up over the back of my head to stop the worst of the damage.

I felt the vibrations quiver through the ground, and I felt every tooth in my mouth shake with the shock of it. And that ringin' in my ears, it just got shriller and shriller till it was almost too much to bear.

But, even with all that ringin', I was just about certain of what I could hear, back there, beyond all that noise, all that background stuff.

I could hear the dozens of screams of all those unquiet souls as they shipped off the face of the universe, and into the beyond . . . or wherever it was they were headed.

15

THE AFTERSHOCKS came thick and fast and I could hear the debris, surely molten hot and fierce-sharp, whistlin' down all round my head. And I heard it drop into the trees, rustlin' the leaves and breakin' branches and all that. The cracklin' of the fire too, and that ever-present stench of smoke that seemed to thicken the air for miles round.

I have no idea how long I lay there with my head to the earth, but I do know that when I finally came round, I could already hear another *thrum* in the air. Even in my state of shock, of my whole body rocking about, and seeming to fly from side to side, despite being laid out on the ground, I knew just what it was.

The rebel ship.

The one that'd shot us down.

That'd *killed* my crew, and my captain.

And my first thought was to get back to Brennant, because I had to do whatever I could for him now, I had to *take care* of him.

As I swung myself back up onto my heels, I made the mistake of taking a glance back to the Pelter, back to good ol' *P-0993c*—God rest her soul—and saw her smouldering away there, just the wreckage of her remaining.

And I knew that no one else had survived.

That was the first time I thought to question me disarming the thermonuke. I mean, surely it woulda meant something to have it go off?

Because, as far as the FSA was concerned, what was the difference to them between havin' a whole crew killed except two, and the mission failed, as opposed to completing the mission and havin' everyone die?

Well, to me, there never seemed another option. And, just as I tell myself to this day, we'd been thrown off course so hard that leaving that thermonuke on Standby, or worse, arming it, might well have meant wiping out a whole, settlement of good-natured civilians.

Civilians that just wanted to live their lives in peace. Just like my family had wanted to live back on Arkle, and had never got a chance. And I knew that it was my intention to come along here and liberate them from these rebels making these good, ordinary people slaves to their ego dreams.

And that I'd failed at that.

But at least they still had their lives. That was somethin'.

———

I made it back to the clearin' where I'd left Brennant all slumped up against the rock. As I rustled my way past the thick foliage, getting scratched up all over my arms, I realised that my chest burned red-hot, and that my heart was beatin' all the quicker.

When I looked down, I saw that the front of my uniform was dark and damp with blood. It took me another second or two to remember that it was my blood.

And then the weakness came, and I felt my

knees shakin', my toes goin' numb, and my blood a runnin' cold.

I swaggered on, and then reached out for the rock, feeling its rough surface beneath my cut-up hands, and then I let myself slump down right beside Brennant.

We didn't say anything, and the *throb* of the rebel's large ship continued to pound through the air, and I knew it was just a matter of time before we got captured. Before they took us to wherever their headquarters were.

And who knew what'd happen to us then?

But there was really nothing else to be done. Best case scenario would be the rebels buzzin' off somewhere else, maybe picking through the wreckage of the *P-0993c*, and then movin' on . . . leavin' me and Brennant to the wolves, or whatever the hell they had here in this forest of theirs.

But they did find us.

16

EVERYTHING TASTED of ash as I lay on my side, feeling the springs of my bed creaking beneath my weight. The mattress I lay on was all stodgy and covered in dark stains. When the pain in my chest got too much to handle I stared at the material first tryin' to work out the colours, to pin them down to some definition, before moving on to think just where those stains mighta come from.

Pretty soon I came up with a tidy list:

Piss, shit, puke, and blood.

More blood than anything else, all told, and counting the stuff I was pumpin' out onto the mattress, that stain was only gettin' all the bigger.

I'd long lost the ability to taste anything any more, I just had that sharp taste of spaceship fuel lingering all over my mouth, all cooped up inside it. Outside I could hear the *whirr* of electrics and the bubblin' of some pipe or other.

But, more than anythin' else, I could still hear those screams.

The screams would start out loud and then get quieter, as if it was the sound of people being tossed into a bottomless pit, arms flailin' out and mouths opened-wide screeching away. And as they'd plunge deeper into that pit their screams would get quieter, and then fade all together.

Then my mind would be at peace, and I'd have a few moments of silence. And then, next thing I'd know, it'd all get to starting over again.

In those brief moments, when I didn't have to clench my eyes shut tight to try and bear those gut-wrenching screams, I glanced out into the gloom of the jail cell, and over to Brennant who lay on the bunk opposite mine.

He slept the whole damn time, the only movement he made was the twitchin' of his fingers, and sometimes his legs. And I could sometimes hear mutterings that died on his lips.

Not that I tried too hard to understand just what they meant.

Because it couldn't be anything positive, nothin' that could be comforting about this situation we found ourselves in.

The air was hot and humid too, and even more so as the night rolled in, and the gloom in the cell became all-out blackness. There was no artificial light in our cell, or out there in the corridor. And, as far as I could see, no guard in sight.

If only I coulda thought of some plan, some masterstroke. But those screams. Those screams kept on comin' back and near enough wrenchin' my skull right open.

I couldn't hardly think for those screams.

I'm not all that certain how long we'd been in that cell when I lost the ability to tell whether the moisture stickin' to my uniform— *soakin'* my uniform—was blood or sweat, but it was most definitely round that time that I heard the footsteps outside the cell, someone out there comin' to visit us.

And I had just seen off another of the iterations of the screamin' when I turned to look at the bars and I saw a light peeking in.

It can't have been all that bright, but it was bright enough to send flashes of pain dancin' through my skull, and my hands shakin' all over. I guessed by that time I needed food and water and medical care.

Well, at least it turned out that the last of those was gonna get taken care of.

––––––

It wasn't till after the doc had left, after he'd patched us up and then cleared out of the cell, leaving us back in that perpetual darkness, that I thought about how I'd wasted the opportunity to get some info out of him.

But, at the time, while he'd been seein' to the wound in my chest, and later the wound on Brennant's head, I'd been so struck first with the screaming voices, and then by the sharp pain of the alcohol meetin' my lashed-up skin that I'd simply forgotten.

Just plain not had the energy to remember.

Not that it mattered all that much, because, as things were soon turning out, this whole situation had very quickly slipped out of our hands. *Both* our hands, for what Brennant actually knew of it, since he spent the whole of our incarceration in that near state of coma.

Yeah, that was how it was. How I got my first proper dose of just how politics on this planet-sized scale truly worked. And I knew that it consisted of leaving the hostages . . . the *widgets* . . . right out of it.

No one even spoke to us as the rebel guards finally made an appearance and I was so lashed out from all the time spent in that dank, dark cell, that I could hardly form words. In fact, thinkin' back on it I mighta said, 'Thank you' to them, even though I had no way of knowing what my fate was to be.

Because I knew, whether I was gonna be executed or freed, that I'd finally never have to return to that jail cell, to be there in that stifling silence and overwhelming heat where I'd be pinned down and forced to hear those screams, over and over again.

17

SOMEWHERE WELL OUT OF MINE and Brennant's earshot the decisions got made, the deals got struck, and next thing he or I knew we were being shipped out on an Extractor and headed right back for the *FSA-0100T*, the mother ship.

Though I remember Brennant being conscious for that journey, all's I remember is that we didn't speak at all. I guess there just wasn't nothing to say. I mean, we knew what had happened, that we'd lost all our beloved crewmembers . . . and we also knew just what had gone on on that bridge, *exactly* what'd gone on there.

And though it was his word against mine, I

knew that when the enquiry rolled round there was no way that I'd be capable of telling them anything other than the truth.

I remember very clearly staring through the porthole, watching us roll about in that Extractor, in that sea-sick motion that it does, and us drawing closer to that enormous opening hatch of the mother ship, and knowing that soon we'd be back inside.

Safe.

————

The hearing was set for about a week later on, after me and Brennant had had a chance to get checked over, after Doctor Sheila Mutely had given us both a good going over, had made sure that we were back to being fighting fit . . . or at least on the road to being so.

Doctor Mutely didn't give no clues away as she checked me over, after she patched up that great big hole in my chest and sorta got things all firing as normal. There was no confidin' look from her this time round, now she was all-business, all the time. And I didn't blame her. Way things were headed I was looking all set for a dishonourable discharge.

And, to be honest, that was most likely all I deserved.

———

Standin' outside in the ersatz oak-panelled hall-way, I felt my heart skip and dip more than I'd ever felt before . . . except perhaps when we'd been plummeting inside the Pelter, headed right for the ground of Orkron-1.

And, truth be told, it didn't have much to do with those admirals all awaitin' inside the towerin' hall, but more to do with those screams, still bouncing back and forth, all about my skull.

But I kept my back straight, ditched my gum in a handy bin and, breath nice and minty fresh, mouth now all *tangy*, I straightened out a crease in the cuff of my dress uniform and then marched right into that hall, chin tilted a little way back, and shoulders squared, just like I'd planned it.

Maybe I was a coward, but at least I'd be a *dignified* coward.

———————

The two men and three ladies all sat in a row, their caps all brought down low over their faces, leaving them in shadow. I could see their expressions were grim, just as the circumstances dictated. It wasn't every day that almost a whole crew of a Pelter got lost.

Or that the FSA found itself bargaining with—*pandering to*—rebel forces for the survivors.

Looking back on things, and seeing past that awful, *awful*, tragedy that'll haunt me till the end of my days, I thought on how the very worst part was that all that loss of human life had been for nothin' at all.

The people of Orkron-1 were just as imprisoned as they had been before and, what was worse, the rebels now had their twitchy, mouldy tails up—they'd feel themselves to be like towering giants . . . the ones that'd seen off an FSA raid, neutralised a thermonuke headed right for their headquarters, and not only lived to tell the tale, but actually struck a deal out of the whole sticky situation.

It woulda been enough to keep me awake at

night . . . if those screams hadn't already done so.

The soles of my well-polished shoes squeaked as they passed along the ersatz porcelain tiles beneath my feet, the squeaking reverberating all about the hall.

And I could once again taste and smell that polish, that *wax*, in the air, the one that always reminded me of how that corridor back on Arkle-4, in our apartment building, had smelled like. It sent a fresh shudder skittering right up my spine.

All subtle, I wiped my gently perspiring hands on the sides of my trousers and kept up my jutted posture, kept that chin raised, as I stepped through that swinging ersatz oak gate and took my place before the five admirals.

———

As I took my place there, I got hit by a fresh bout of nausea. Why, it just rippled right through my gut and sent my head spinnin'. I reached out for the ersatz wooden back of the dock . . . or whatever the hell this thing I was inside was called . . . and steadied myself.

One of the female admirals, the one sat in the centre, and who I realised soon enough was the *Lead* Admiral of the whole fleet: Lead Admiral Hulzberk, leaned forwards from her place and asked, in a stern, even voice, "Lieutenant Wright, are you feeling well?"

I steeled myself, arched my shoulders just a little more, and then looked her right back in the eye. Because I'd be *damned* if I wasn't gonna go through with this. Now was the time. I had to stand up and face the music—be a man. Account for what I'd done, the decisions . . . the *in*action I'd committed.

"Yes, ma'am," I replied. "Perfectly fine," I added, feeling just about anything but.

In fact, I found myself scouring the room with my gaze tryin' my best to locate the nearest bin to be sick into if I felt the driving need.

"Okay then," she said, "then we'll begin." She cocked her head to the side, and addressed the man standing in the dock to the side of me, the man that I only realised right then had bright red hair. "You may go now, Officer Brennant."

As Brennant stepped down from his place,

and headed out through that swinging gate, he didn't make to catch my eye. I looked to where they'd patched him up—where Doctor Mutely had patched him up—and I wondered just what he'd said about me.

The doors to the hall swung shut behind Brennant, and Lead Admiral Hulzberk spoke again. "Lieutenant Wright, we have been hearing the details of the case for the past few hours, and have just finished hearing the testimony of your crewmate Officer Brennant. It now falls to you to give your own accounting of events as you witnessed them from your point of view."

I wouldn't be a man if I didn't admit, just for the most fleetin' of seconds, that I sincerely flirted with the idea of tellin' a lie. Of making out my role to be any different from surely what Brennant had told them, and goin' at it man-to-man, eye-witness against eye-witness.

I knew I could save my career if I really wanted.

But, from somewhere, deep in my gut . . . maybe some would call it a *soul*, but I really wouldn't go that far . . . I knew just what I had to tell them.

And so I did.

———

With my account all finished, after tellin' them from start to end just how it'd all played out, I sat back on my heels and skirted my eyes over the five admirals all seated up there, a solid head and shoulders above me.

They conferred among one another, and I really had no idea just what I was supposed to do next. I glanced back over my shoulder wondering if I was meant to just scurry on out, head back to my bunk, and wait for just what they had to say.

Just as I was on the cusp of beatin' a retreat for the exit, of headin' right out of that hall to wait for the news on my discharge . . . and surely my FSA-sponsored return to Arkle-4 . . . Lead Admiral Hulzberk cleared her throat and started into me again.

"One thing, Lieutenant, just one thing we'd like to get clarified." She tapped away at some screen out of my sight there on the bench before her, the thing that I guessed she'd been recording all my testimony into. Some piece of technocrap.

"Ma'am?" I said.

"Your *freezing*, as you put it. When Captain Hughes requested that you go to the back of the ship and fix the afterburners. That was missing from Officer Brennant's account, and we'd just like you to confirm what you've said before this board of enquiry is, to the best of your recollection, truthful."

My heart skipped several beats. My mind bucked a little, and I knew that this would be my chance, my *final* chance, to keep myself in the FSA. If I could just smudge the truth, just a little, my career would be assured.

But there was no way I could.

If I had tried it would've been to discredit all those lost lives.

All my dead brothers and sisters in arms.

"Completely as I remembered, ma'am," I replied a second or so later.

Lead Admiral Hulzberk leaned back in her chair and eyed me through those thin-framed glasses of hers, and she rapped her fingers against the bench before her, making a kinda low rumbling sound.

A sound that, somehow, made me flinch. Reminded me of the crash.

But, then again, *everything* seemed to remind me of the crash.

"That will be all, Lieutenant," she said, and turned back to the screen before her, up there on the bench out of my line of sight.

18

I FELT a kind of condemned man those days waitin' for the decision to get made. First thing I tried was to pin down just where Officer Brennant had got to, and to thank him for not telling the board about how I'd frozen up and all. It was the least I could do knowing that he musta felt something terrible about having such an incompetent as myself promoted ahead of him to Lieutenant, and to have cost the Pelter in such a way.

But, from what I gathered, Brennant had been transferred out, sent to another mother ship. And I couldn't help thinkin', speculatin' about whether it mighta been for me. That they mighta been worried that I'd go after Brennant when they finally discharged me, as if it'd been something that he'd done to get me that discharge.

And so I waited out the time till I got message through that I was to go before the board of enquiry yet again, that I was to go don my dress uniform again, go stand up there and receive my punishment.

As if those screams I heard rattle through my skull every night . . . in every dream . . . every nightmare . . . weren't enough punishment to serve me a lifetime.

————

I got a little struck down with the déjà vu as I trod those porcelain tiles yet again, and I entered back into that dock, and stood right in front of those poutin' admirals for another turn. And I felt my gut getting all wrenched up, and that nausea seeping back into my blood and bones. But I was gettin' better. I was gettin' over my shock, as Doctor Mutely had put it. And soon enough I'd be back to something like normal, though it seemed like I'd never be anywhere near to normal again for as long as I lived.

Lead Admiral Hulzberk was the one that spoke again, and I couldn't help thinkin' that the way she spoke, the tone she struck, made me think of a funeral.

And, in a way, it was.

Because after all the funerals for all my fallen crewmembers had been done and dusted, now it would turn to the funeral of my professional career.

"Lieutenant Wright, the decision which this board of enquiry has reached has been based on both you and your fellow crewmember, Officer Brennant's, testimony, along with that logged on the communicators for the duration of the raid on Orkron-1, otherwise referenced under the code: ORK0023, the dialogue kept open by Captain Hughes until the moment of impact."

My gut wrenched just a little more at the mention of Captain Hughes's name, and I was sure, just for the shred of a second, that among all those other screams pounding in my skull, I could hear his scream . . . like he'd taken centre stage and he was standin' there, takin' his solo.

"Have you any other information you would like this board to consider before you are informed of the final decision?"

I swallowed hard and tried to keep the waverin' out of my voice . . . or at least to keep it just as mute as I could. "No, ma'am," I said.

"Then it's to this board's will that it recommends you for Special Commendation for Surviving Enemy Capture, Not Collaborating with the Enemy, and for Outstanding Service in the Most Extreme of Circumstances."

My gut dropped right down and I was sure that, just for a moment, the wax in the hall got all overwhelming. And then I seemed to catch up with myself, to try and rationalise the Lead Admiral's words as far as I could . . . to bring myself back down to earth, as much as I could be standing on earth in this mother ship.

Most likely this would be a golden goodbye. Something embarrassing that the FSA just wanted swept under the carpet, prim and proper, before anyone started asking too many uncomfortable questions about the nature of the mission.

And so I stood my ground and waited for the rest of what the Lead Admiral had to say.

"Furthermore," she continued, "on the basis of your outstanding service, and the commendations forthcoming, the board recommends a promotion to the rank of Captain." She paused a long, pregnant moment, and I felt those eyeballs of hers, bobbin' about beneath the lenses of her glasses, linger over me, make my skin twitch, then she added, "Following a short period for recuperation, of course."

I suppose the whole purpose of the Lead Admiral's talk was to get me feelin' better, but, to be honest, it only made things worse. I'd spent the whole of that week, the whole time since I'd got back, actually, just furrowin' and fawnin' over what I was gonna do once I got dishonourably discharged and sent right back to Arkle-4.

Now, though, this was different. *This* was somethin' that I'd never thought might come true in my wildest of dreams . . . when those dreams weren't drowned out by the screams, that is.

It was like some invisible person or thing was scrapin' the words right off my tongue before I even got the chance to say them, to float them out there into the air in front of my nose. And that knot in my gut just got tighter as I tried to speak.

Lead Admiral Hulzberk eyeballed me some more, and that trademark pout of hers— of *all* of the board of enquiry—got a little thinner before eventually twitchin' out into a smile.

"This wasn't a simple decision to take, Lieutenant Wright," she said. "This was something that was taken with great deliberation and, believe me, the board is perfectly aware of your age, and that this appointment would make you the youngest captain in the Fritten System Authorities. But it was also the only decision the board felt to be advisable, given your commendations and your service record thus far in the FSA."

My heart wrenched, and suddenly tried to make a go at bustin' right out through my ribs. I actually held my hands up to my chest as if that might be a real possibility.

It did stay put, though.

She looked me over a little more then said, "Do you have anything to say, *Cap*-tain Wright?"

This time I did manage to get a hold on one

of those squirmy words, and I delivered it just fine. "Just 'thank you,' ma'am."

She gave me another of those wry smiles of hers, and then said, "Captain Wright, the board of enquiry hereby dismisses you."

"Thank you, ma'am," I just about got out as I shoved right through the spring-bound gate and pattered on out of the hall.

———

That night in my bunk, I spent a lot of time thinkin'. Which is to say, for me, to spend any time thinkin' at all . . . why it was pretty much a minor miracle. The way that everything had played out, why it just seemed all-round strange to me. Almost impossible to understand.

All I could think of was that moment, where I'd been sittin' up in my chair, in that *imposter's* chair, right up beside Captain Hughes, and how when they'd needed me more than ever, to go off and sort out the afterburners, all I'd been able to do was get lost in a daze and think back to them times back on Arkle-4.

Was that where I really should be?

Perhaps it was.

Because I knew, if Captain Hughes had been on the board, if he'd have been alive to give his own testimony, that he would've told them just what a liability I was. There would be no commendation, there would be no promotion, and I'd have been cast out from the FSA, sent packin' right back to the backwater where I'd come from.

And I knew now that it was my duty to do the right thing. I had to look at myself, ask myself if I truly was a captain, if I could *really* promise myself not to freeze up all over again, like I did on the bridge of the Pelter.

Now *there* was a promise I simply couldn't make.

So, with my mind made up, I hauled myself up off my bunk, and traipsed my way off along the corridor. I guess I hadn't much idea just where I was headed till I found myself facin' off with a security officer, the man who stood guardin' the entrance to the admirals' quarters.

I asked to see Lead Admiral Hulzberk. And after a brief bit of resistance, he let me on through, even showed me the way to her office.

————

I told her all about the whole deal, feelings and all. And she sat back in her chair eyein' me closely, and, I could tell, absorbin' not just the words but the way I said them too. I did my best to get my case across though there's never really any tellin' for certain just how it fell on her ears.

When I'd got done with the whole thing, she unhooked her glasses from behind her ears, and she laid them down on the desk in front of her, then said, "Well, Captain Wright, what is it that you'd like us to do?"

I breathed in a couple of times, and it felt good, refreshing. I was startin' to lose all that smoke that'd hung about inside me now, and beginnin' to feel like my normal self again. My normal, *coward* self.

"Ma'am, I hate to say it, but I can't but tell the truth, if you get my meaning?"

She nodded slightly.

"I think it'd be for the best of everyone if you just got shot of me, if you just sent me off back home."

And with that, the words hung in the air,

never able to be unsaid. I watched as Lead Admiral Hulzberk wrung her hands, her knobbly finger joints movin' silently beneath her paper-thin skin.

"It'd be a real shame to lose you, Wright," she said. "But if that's how you feel, then I don't think there's any other way to go about it." She stared down at her well-polished, ersatz mahogany desk, and I saw her ghostly reflection starin' right back up at her. "Oh, I'll make sure you're discharged with great honour and everything like that, because, unlike yourself, I do appreciate your efforts on the raid, even if you do not."

I felt a slight warmth in my chest, and the hollow echoes of the screams in my head dulled just for a second.

"And as for sending you home, wouldn't it make more sense to put you on a half-salary, until you find your feet, until you've had some time off, and then you can make the decision on your future, whether you wish to continue with the FSA or not?"

"That would be wonderful, ma'am," I said, feeling that glowing warmth grow through my chest and begin to warm my blood.

I wouldn't have to go back to Arkle-4, if I didn't want.

I waited to see if she had anything else to say. She was one of those people that seemed perpetually on the brink of sayin' something. And so I waited there, all quiet, and ready to hear out whatever she said.

"It's impossible to know," she said, "just what it must have been like, having gone through what you've gone through. And you must understand that, however you might analyse these events, however you might play them back in your mind years from now, that it wasn't your fault."

Her stare seemed to fizzle right through me, and I felt my heart leapin' all about inside because I knew what she was sayin', that it simply wasn't true. That she *hadn't* been there. That she wouldn't need to be the one that had to live with it.

Her eyes left mine, and she looked down to the back of her hand. "No," she said, "the buck goes further up the chain." She met my eye again. "And it stops with me. *I* am the one that's responsible, you must understand that."

"Yes, ma'am," I replied.

She put on a hardy smile and rose from her chair. She reached across the table and took my hand in hers. We shared a brisk handshake, and then she said, "Good luck, Captain Wright, and don't forget that there will *always* be a place for you here at the FSA just as long as you need it."

"Thank you, ma'am, that means a lot to me."

Another smile and then she nodded to the door, and I took my hint, and took my leave.

19

A FEW MONTHS LATER I had everything just about sorted. Of course I had no intention of livin' on the hand outs the FSA fed me the rest of my life. I knew that I had to make my own way. I'd made that decision the moment that I'd left Arkle-4. So I bought myself a ship with the credits they gave me and took on whatever jobs I could pick up: shippin' stuff here, ferryin' people there, and such.

And I made some pretty good money.

Good enough money that I could pay back the money the FSA had donated to me, and so that I could let them stop giving me that pension, or whatever they called those payments they were making out to me.

They didn't have to worry about me any more.

I named the ship the *Navaplastas*, and took to space barrelling about here and there, and always thinking back on those kind words Lead Admiral Hulzberk had given me. Those words that, really, she'd never had to say at all.

But I appreciated them all the same, though I couldn't think to believe them entirely.

Because Lead Admiral Hulzberk never had to hear those screams in her dreams, never had to smell that lingering, thick smoke or taste that ash on her tongue. Never heard those alarms wailing out. And never had to live with having failed to follow a captain's direct order, having frozen up when she mighta been able to save the whole ship—to save everyone's soul on board the ship.

But that was stuff that *I'd* have to go on livin' with from now on.

After a while, maybe five years or so of bumming about the universe, I noticed those nightmares slackenin' off a little, and those screams growin' somewhat quieter. And it was then that I learned that I was gonna be able to live with myself, that I *was* gonna be able to go on livin'.

But I also knew that I would never quite shake those screams entirely, that they'd never completely go away, and, in some way, I was glad about that.

Because that way I would never forget completely all those unquiet souls.

AUTHOR'S NOTE

Thank you for taking the time to read one of my books. If you would like to hear about my latest releases you can sign up for my newsletter here: www.raymondsflex.com

Thanks for reading!

Raymond S Flex

All These Unquiet Souls
An Arkle Wright Novella